THE DRAGON WITH THE BLAZING BOTTOM

A VERY FIERY FAIRY TALE

SIMON & SCHUSTER

London   New York   Sydney   Toronto   New Delhi

For James, Katie & Lucy

Edited by Polly Whybrow &
Designed by Chloë Bilalis

Simon & Schuster
First published in Great Britain in 2021 by Simon & Schuster UK Ltd
1st Floor, 222 Gray's Inn Road, London, WC1X 8HB
Text & illustration copyright © 2021 Beach

A CIP catalogue record for this book is available
from the British Library upon request
ISBNs: 978-1-3985-0639-8 (HB) 978-1-4711-9722-2 (PB)
978-1-4711-9723-9 (eB)
Printed in Great Britain
by Bell & Bain Ltd, Glasgow
3 5 7 9 10 8 6 4

MIX
Paper from
responsible sources
FSC
www.fsc.org   FSC® C007785

Dragon was up bright and early one day,
Fighting Sir Wayne in a fearsome display.

Stomping and chomping, he romped on and on,
When all of a sudden . . .

something was wrong.

He huffed and he puffed with all of his might,
But nothing caught fire –
no knight was alight.

"Lost your spark?"
said Sir Wayne.
"Probably flu.
No need to worry –
still lots you can do."

"There's howling
and scowling,
and thrashing your tail,

Or roaring and clawing –
that never fails.

How about frowning
as hard as you can?"

"STOP!" said Dragon. "Don't you know who I am?
Fire-Breathing Dragon. The clue's in the name.
When I breathe on a knight,
I expect to see flame!"

DRAGON,
FIRE-BREATHING
Infammus
Inflammus

"In that case," said Wayne, "open them wide."
So Dragon said, "Aaaaaah," and the knight peered inside.

"Oh dear, oh dear.
Oh dear, deary me."

"What is it?" gasped Dragon. "What can you see?"

"Your teeth," Wayne said slowly, "are MUCH too clean.

And as for your tongue,
it's the pinkest I've seen!

Your breath still smells bad,
but not bad enough.

I don't think you're eating quite the right stuff."

Sir Wayne struck a pose, as only knights can.
"Fear not," he declared, "for I have a plan!"

"I know a recipe so scorching hot,
The last batch I made burned
right through the pot."

"Sounds perfect," said Dragon. "Just what I need.
A fry-up THAT fired-up is bound to succeed."

So Wayne took his quill and wrote a prescription:
"One hot dinner to match this description . . .

"... Eight zappy eels, the electrical kind.
Six sacks of coal, all the oil you can find.
Two hundred fireflies, a flaming log fire,
A huge spiky cactus,
wrapped in barbed wire.

A heat-seeking rocket, one burning bush,
Sparklers and fireworks, the ones that go . . .

WHOOSH!

And last but not least . . .
a small chunk of cheese –
Almost as green as the snot
from a sneeze."

The pot fizzed and flashed, every drop blazing.

"Wow!" shouted Dragon.
"This looks AMAZING!"

He picked up the dish
and swallowed the lot.

"Flaming flip-flops!" he cried.
"That's hit the spot.

You best grab a shield,
    my tiny tin squire.
        Big Bad Dragon is about to BREATHE FIRE."

So he summoned his strength with a deafening roar . . .

. . . But his breath was still flameless,
just as before . . .

"No, no, wait – your armour's too good.
I can't burn metal – I should have tried wood."

So he blew on a log . . .
But that was too big.

Then he blew on a branch.

And a stick.

And a twig.

But every time his breath was the same,
No puff of black smoke, no hint of a flame.

Dragon collapsed in a heap on the floor.
"I'm all blown out. I can't blow any more.
It's over," he sighed. "I'll have to retire.
I can't be a dragon if I can't breathe fire."

"Please," said Sir Wayne, "don't feel so deflated.
Setting knights on fire is way overrated.
You're so much more than a bonfire with wings.
You've a heart that soars and a soul that sings.

And . . ."

He stopped.

Dragon, it seemed, was no longer listening.
One of his nostrils had just started whistling . . .

. . . His teeth flashed red. Both ears were aglow.
Hot scales blew steam from his head to his toes.

Giant sparks danced on every claw.
And from deep inside came a rumbling roar.

"FIRE!" yelled Dragon – a glint in his eyes.
But he and Sir Wayne were due a surprise.

Just at the moment when flames should appear,
He heard a strange noise away to his rear.

Dragon, it seemed,
had set light to a cart,
With a fearfully, flamefully, dragonly . . .

"My goodness," said Wayne, holding his nose,
"I wasn't expecting to see one of those.

Still, better out than in, I always say.
A bot that hot will scare most knights away."

So though it comes out not quite as before,
Dragon has fire in his belly once more.

And the truth of our tale is plain to see –

Don't stand behind dragons
just after tea.